I LIKE ME!

NANCY CARLSON

Puffin Books

Dedicated to Nell
Tucker, Minnow AND
Anne of Fish Creek.

PUFFIN BOOKS
Published by the Penguin Group
Penguin Putnam Books for Young Readers, 345 Hudson Street,
New York, New York 10014, U.S.A.
Penguin Books Ltd, 27 Wrights Lane, London W8 5TZ, England
Penguin Books Australia Ltd, Ringwood, Victoria, Australia
Penguin Books Canada Ltd, 10 Alcorn Avenue, Toronto, Ontario, Canada M4V 3B2
Penguin Books (N.Z.) Ltd, 182-190 Wairau Road, Auckland 10, New Zealand

Penguin Books Ltd, Registered Offices: Harmondsworth, Middlesex, England

First published in the United States of America by Viking Penguin,
a division of Penguin Books USA Inc., 1988
Published in Picture Puffins, 1990
25 27 29 30 28 26 24
Copyright © Nancy Carlson, 1988
All rights reserved

LIBRARY OF CONGRESS CATALOGING IN PUBLICATION DATA
Carlson, Nancy L.   I like me! / Nancy Carlson.   p.   cm.
Summary: By admiring her finer points and showing that she can
take care of herself and have fun even when there's no one else
around, a charming pig proves the best friend you can have is yourself.
ISBN 0-14-050819-8
[1. Pigs—Fiction.   2. Self-reliance—Fiction.]   I. Title.
[PZ7.C21665Iab 1990]   [E]—dc20   89-36024

Printed in Hong Kong
Set in Century Schoolbook

I have a best friend.

That best friend is me!

I do fun things with me.

I draw beautiful pictures.

I ride fast!

And I read good books with me!

I like to take care of me.

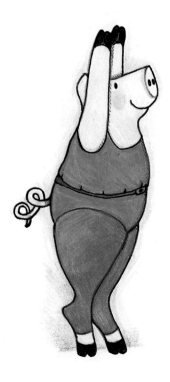

I brush my teeth.

I keep clean and

I eat good food.

When I get up in the morning

I say, "Hi, good-looking!"

I like my curly tail,

my round tummy,

and my tiny little feet.

When I feel bad,

I cheer myself up.

When I fall down,

I pick myself up.

When I make mistakes,

I try

and

try   again!

No matter where I go,

or what I do,

I'll always be me, and

I like that!!!